Dink, Josh, and Ruth Rose aren't the only kid detectives!

What about you?

Can you find the hidden message inside this book?

There are 26 illustrations in this book, not counting the one on the title page, the map at the beginning, or the picture of the jack-o'-lantern that repeats at the start of many of the chapters. In each of the 26 illustrations, there's a hidden letter. If you can find all the letters, you will spell out a secret message!

If you're stumped, the answer is on the bottom of page 132.

Happy detecting!

This book is dedicated to parents who read to their children.
—R.R.

To the residents of the real Tarrytown, New York,
all of whom have level heads on their shoulders
—J.S.G.

Text copyright © 2010 by Ron Roy
Illustrations and map copyright © 2010 by John Steven Gurney

All rights reserved.
Published in the United States by Random House Children's Books,
a division of Random House, Inc., New York.

Random House and the colophon and A to Z Mysteries are registered trademarks and
A Stepping Stone Book and the colophon and the A to Z Mysteries colophon are
trademarks of Random House, Inc.

Visit us on the Web!
www.randomhouse.com/kids

Educators and librarians, for a variety of teaching tools, visit us at
www.randomhouse.com/teachers

Library of Congress Cataloging-in-Publication Data
Roy, Ron.
Sleepy Hollow sleepover / by Ron Roy ; illustrated by John Steven Gurney. — 1st ed.
    p. cm. — (A to Z mysteries super edition ; #4)
"A Stepping Stone book."
Summary: Dink, Josh, and Ruth Rose are enjoying Halloween fun in Sleepy Hollow,
New York, but when unplanned spooky things start happening, they investigate
whether a real headless horseman might be to blame.
ISBN 978-0-375-86669-2 (trade) — ISBN 978-0-375-96669-9 (lib. bdg.) —
ISBN 978-0-375-89829-7 (e-book)
[1. Mystery and detective stories. 2. Halloween—Fiction. 3. Robbers and outlaws—
Fiction. 4. Sleepy Hollow (N.Y.)—Fiction.] I. Gurney, John Steven, ill. II. Irving,
Washington, 1783–1859. Legend of Sleepy Hollow. III. Title.
PZ7.R8139Sl 2010
[Fic]—dc22
2009052930

Printed in the United States of America

10 9 8 7 6 5 4 3 2 1

A to Z Mysteries

Super Edition #4

Sleepy Hollow Sleepover

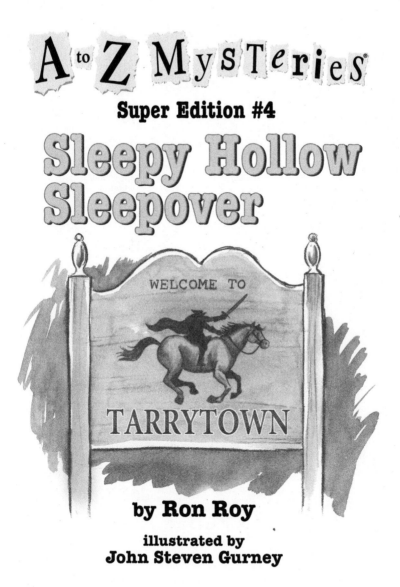

WELCOME TO

TARRYTOWN

by Ron Roy

illustrated by
John Steven Gurney

A STEPPING STONE BOOK™

Random House 🏠 New York

CHAPTER 1

"Starting today, I'm changing my ice cream flavor," Josh said. He was staring into the Sweet Youth Ice Cream Shop window. "From now on, I'm only eating raspberry!"

"But you always choose pistachio," Dink said. "I've known you five years, and it's pistachio every time."

Josh shrugged. "I guess I'm tired of green," he said.

Ruth Rose poked the boys. "How about *that* green, Josh?" she asked. "Green money!"

An armored truck had pulled up to

the bank, next to the ice cream shop. Three men wearing dark green uniforms unloaded bags of money onto a cart. Two of the guards pushed the cart through the glass doors into the bank. The third man watched over the truck.

Josh grinned. "Can't I have red ice cream and green money?" he asked.

Dink, Josh, and Ruth Rose were in Tarrytown, New York. It was Halloween day, and families from all over had come to Tarrytown for a big party and haunted hayride. Dink watched some kids and their parents enter the ice cream shop next to the bank.

The guards came out of the bank with the empty cart, climbed into the truck, and drove away.

Ruth Rose walked to the bank window. She tapped a finger against the glass. "This hayride is going to be so cool!" she said.

The kids read the sign hanging inside the window. It said:

DON'T MISS THE HAUNTED HAYRIDE
AND HALLOWEEN PARTY TONIGHT!
FOOD, GAMES, A BONFIRE,
AND LOTS OF SPOOKY STUFF!
AND WATCH OUT FOR THE
HEADLESS HORSEMAN!
HE'LL BE WATCHING YOU!

In the window, behind the sign, stood a big brown horse. A curtain separated the horse from the rest of the bank. The kids knew that the horse was fake, but it looked real. On top of the horse sat a dummy of a man dressed in black. A cloak hung from his shoulders. But his head was missing.

"How can the headless horseman be watching us?" Josh asked. "The dude has no eyes! Who is that guy, anyway?"

Ruth Rose opened her book bag. In it were her Swiss Army knife, a couple of books, and her cell phone. She pulled out a guidebook for New York State and opened to the pages about Tarrytown.

"Listen to this," she said. "A writer named Washington Irving wrote a story called 'The Legend of Sleepy Hollow.' It was about a schoolteacher named Ichabod Crane who lived here, in Tarrytown. He was—"

"Hey, I saw that movie!" Josh said.

"Yeah, but first it was a book, Josh," Dink said. "Keep reading, Ruth Rose."

"Anyway, this teacher was in love with a woman named Katrina," Ruth Rose went on. "But some other guy loved her, too. His name was Brom Bones. So in the story, Mr. Bones dressed up as a headless horseman to scare Ichabod Crane out of town."

"Did it work?" Josh asked.

Ruth Rose read more. "Yup. Old Ichabod mysteriously disappeared, and Katrina married Brom Bones."

"But it was all fake, right?" Josh asked. "There really was no headless horseman?"

Ruth Rose read some more. "Brom Bones didn't want anyone to know that he was the headless horseman. So he told people it was the ghost of a soldier who had lost his head in a battle," she said. "And at night, his ghost rides around Tarrytown looking for the head!"

"Gross!" Josh cried.

"Look, guys," Dink said, pointing at the window. A woman had stepped out from behind the curtain. She opened a hidden door in the side of the horse. The woman reached an arm inside the horse, then pulled it back out. She disappeared behind the curtain again.

Suddenly the horse's head moved up and down. Then the legs and feet started pumping in place. The man on the horse's back leaned forward, like a jockey in a race. One hand began slapping the horse with a small whip. The horse looked like it was running!

"This is so awesome!" Ruth Rose said. "It's a mechanical horse!" She handed her book to Dink, pulled out her cell phone, and snapped a bunch of pictures.

A crowd of people had gathered to watch the horse and rider. One little boy started to cry. "That's a scary man!" he said.

The boy's father scooped him up. "It's not real, Simon," the man said. "It's just a big action figure. That man is only a stuffed doll."

"He's scary and I hate him!" Simon howled. "And I want ice cream now!"

The man laughed, then carried the

little boy into the ice cream shop.

"We're looking at our own private piñata," a quiet voice said from behind Dink. Dink glanced at the window and saw a reflection of two men. They wore dark glasses and baseball caps.

"Yeah, and tomorrow Bonnie will fill it with green candy!" the man's buddy said.

After a few minutes, the mechanical horse began to slow down. Finally, it stopped moving altogether. The crowd of people drifted away.

"That was so cool," Ruth Rose said.

"He's scary and I hate him!" Josh whined, sounding just like little Simon. "And I want ice cream now!"

Dink laughed.

As the three kids backed away from the window, Dink stepped on someone's toes. "Sorry," he said.

He turned to the two men he had

overheard talking about a piñata.

"No problem, kid," one of the men said. He pointed to his feet. He was wearing cowboy boots with silver toes. "Nothing can hurt these."

The man's friend pulled on his arm. "Come on, Ace, we have work to do."

Ace and his friend walked away.

"Come on," Josh said, mimicking the man's gruff voice. "We have ice cream to do!" He pulled Dink and Ruth Rose into the ice cream shop.

CHAPTER 2

Licking their ice cream cones, the kids walked to the edge of town. They took a footpath that led into a forest. The tall trees blocked out the October sun.

"How's the new flavor?" Ruth Rose asked Josh. She had chosen strawberry, her favorite. Dink's cone was maple walnut.

"My brain thinks it's okay," Josh said. "But my tongue keeps expecting to taste pistachio."

Dink poked Josh. "What brain?"

Josh poked him back. "The brain that's going to whip you in Monopoly tonight," he said.

"We won't have time to finish a whole game," Ruth Rose said. She glanced at her watch. "It's almost five o'clock, and the hayride is at seven."

Josh pushed out his chest. "The way I play, I'll be rich by six-thirty!" he boasted.

They were staying with Dink's father in a small cabin in the forest. A few other families had rented cabins, too. Each cabin was named after something creepy. Dink's dad had chosen one called Haunted House. The name was painted on a sign on the front porch railing.

When they reached the cabin, Dink's father was sitting in a rocking chair on the porch. An open book was in his lap.

"Hey, kids," he said as they approached. "How was town?"

"A lot of other kids are here for the hayride," Ruth Rose told him.

"And we saw a headless horseman, only it was fake," Josh said.

"What're you reading, Dad?" Dink asked.

His father held up the book. "It's a history of Tarrytown and Sleepy Hollow," he said.

"Is there really a headless horseman who rides around looking for his head?" Josh asked Mr. Duncan.

"Why, I believe there is," Dink's father answered. He pointed to a map in his book. "This is the area we're in right now. According to legend, this is where the original headless horseman scared Ichabod Crane out of town."

"Aw, Mr. Duncan, you're messing with me, right?" Josh asked.

Dink's father grinned. "Would I tease you, Josh?" he asked.

"Come on," Dink said. "If we're going to play Monopoly, we should get started."

"You kids hungry?" Dink's father asked. "Oh, never mind. I see ice cream on your lips."

"Yeah, Josh whined until we bought him some," Dink said.

Inside the cabin, Dink went toward a small chest under a window. Painted on its side was the word GAMES. He opened the chest, and a skeleton popped up.

"Oh my gosh!" Dink yelled, jumping back.

Josh and Ruth Rose laughed. They ran around the cabin pulling open drawers and peeking inside cupboards and closets. They found a witch in a closet, a bunch of fake bats in a drawer, and a goblin in the bathroom.

"Dad, who did all this?" Dink asked his father.

"Maybe the headless horseman got in here," his dad said in a creepy voice. "I wonder what he put inside your sleeping bags!" He crumpled some paper and started a fire in the fireplace.

"Ha!" Josh said. He glanced at their three sleeping bags stacked in a corner.

The kids finally found the Monopoly game. They set it up on the floor in front of the crackling fire.

A half hour later, Dink looked up. "Did you hear something?" he asked the others.

"Don't try to change the subject," Josh said. "You're losing big-time!"

"I'm not changing the subject," Dink said. "I heard something, like running feet."

Dink got up and walked over to the window. It had grown dark outside. He saw his reflection in the glass and the flickering flames of the fire behind him.

He heard it again, a thudding noise. Then he saw a light among the dark trees. "Guys, come here!" he said.

Dink's father, Josh, and Ruth Rose joined him at the window.

"What is it, son?" Dink's father asked.

"I saw a light," Dink whispered. "It was moving through the trees."

"If you're messing around, I . . . ," Josh started to say. Then he gasped.

A horse raced out of the trees, past the cabin window. A rider carrying a jack-o'-lantern sat on the horse's back.

The horse stopped, and the rider held the jack-o'-lantern high in the air.

"What on earth is anyone doing riding around in the dark?" Dink's father asked.

Dink noticed the flowing cloak, just like on the rider he'd seen in the bank window. Only this one wasn't fake. This was a real man and a real horse.

Then Dink looked above the man's shoulders. There was nothing there.

"I think he's looking for his head," Dink whispered.

"IT'S THE HEADLESS HORSEMAN!" Ruth Rose screamed in Josh's ear.

"Lock the door!" Josh wailed.

"No way!" Ruth Rose said. She grabbed her cell phone. "I'm getting a picture of this!"

"I'll go with you," Dink said. "Coming, Josh?"

"Not for a million dollars!" Josh said.

CHAPTER 3

Dink and Ruth Rose ran outside. They were just in time to see the headless horseman gallop past. Ruth Rose held up her phone and snapped a picture.

The horse and rider disappeared into the trees.

"Did you get the picture?" Dink asked.

"I don't know," Ruth Rose said. She hit a few buttons on her phone. "Look, I just got a blur. He was going too fast."

They headed back to the cabin. Josh opened the door and peeked out. He looked scared.

"Don't worry, he's gone," Ruth Rose said.

"So am I!" Josh said. "Where's the phone? I'm calling a taxi!"

Dink laughed. "Josh, we're in the middle of the woods," he said. "A taxi would charge a ton of money to come out here. And you don't have any money. Remember, I had to pay for your ice cream today."

"Then I'll walk home," Josh said. "I'm not staying where guys with no heads hang out. Mr. Duncan, how far is it back to Green Lawn?"

"Over a hundred miles, Josh," Dink's father said. "It would take you until tomorrow night to make it home."

Ruth Rose grinned. "If some bear didn't eat you first!" she said. "I heard there are lots of bears in these woods."

"Then I'll hitchhike," Josh said.

"Maybe a certain guy on a certain

horse will pick you up," Dink said wickedly.

"You guys aren't scaring me," Josh said.

Dink, his father, and Ruth Rose just looked at Josh.

Josh grinned. "Okay, you *are* scaring me!"

"Josh, do you really think that guy had no head?" Dink asked.

"I saw him, Dinkus," Josh said. "There was nothing above his collar!"

"It must have been a trick," Ruth Rose said. "His head was probably tucked down inside his cape, where we couldn't see it."

"The hayride wagon should be here soon," Dink's father said. He poked the fire and picked up his book. The kids went back to the Monopoly board.

"You landed on one of my hotels!" Josh cried a few minutes later. He grinned at Dink. "You owe me two thousand dollars!"

Dink groaned and counted his money. "I only have about four hundred," he said.

"You'll have to finish the game later," Dink's father said. He stood and glanced out the window. "The wagon is here."

"Yay!" Dink yelled.

Ruth Rose grabbed three masks from a table next to the sofa. She, Dink, and Josh had decided to get Three Stooges masks. She was Larry, Dink was Curly, and Josh had chosen the Moe mask.

"Take your sweaters," Dink's father said. "It'll get colder tonight."

The kids pulled on their sweaters and their masks and ran to open the door. A wagon stood in the clearing in front of the cabin steps. The wagon was piled with hay, and a few kids were lying in it.

A big, long-legged workhorse was hitched to the wagon. It had a droopy mane and huge feet. A driver wearing a big coat and floppy hat sat up front, holding the reins.

A girl popped out of the hay and smiled down at Dink, Josh, and Ruth Rose. She was dressed as a cowgirl. "I like your masks," she said. "Come on up! There's a ladder in the back."

"Call me when you get to the party,"

Dink's father said. "Driver, what time will you bring them back?"

"Ten o'clock," the driver said. His voice was deep, like it came from a hollow place.

Dink shivered. Something about this driver was strange. Was it just his deep voice? And why wouldn't he look at them?

Dink walked to the back of the wagon. Josh and Ruth Rose had already climbed up and were half buried in the hay pile.

Dink found the ladder and joined the other kids in the hay. He flopped on his back and took off his mask. He looked up at the moon shining through the trees and took a deep breath. The hay smelled sweet, like a kitten's breath.

"I'm Candy," the girl said. "And these are my brothers, Adam and Andy. We're from New York City."

One of the boys wore a black mask that covered his eyes, ears, forehead, and hair. The top part of the mask had small, pointy ears. The other brother's mask covered just his eyes.

"I'm Batman," said the first boy. He pointed at his brother. "That's Andy. He's supposed to be Robin, my trusty sidekick!"

Andy grinned. Above his mask, he had pieces of hay stuck in his curly blond hair.

Dink, Josh, and Ruth Rose introduced themselves. "We're from Green Lawn, Connecticut," Dink said.

"We were here last year, too," Adam said. He was tall and lanky, with a wide grin.

The horse plodded through the woods. After a few minutes, it stopped next to a tree. Halfway up the trunk, Dink saw a wide black hole. The driver reached over and thumped the trunk with a pole he'd had on the seat next to him.

Suddenly an explosion of black flying objects erupted from the hole. High-pitched squeaking filled the air around the wagon. Dink saw, heard, and felt hundreds of bats darting past him into the night.

"DIVE!" Ruth Rose screamed. The six kids buried themselves in the hay. Dink could hear giggling and felt the hay scratching his face.

Then they heard the driver laughing. The wagon lurched forward, and once more the horse trudged along.

"You planned that, right?" Josh asked the driver. Like the other kids on the wagon, Josh had hay stuck in his hair.

The driver didn't answer. He flicked the horse's neck with the reins.

The horse continued walking forward, not at all bothered by the bats.

Josh crawled back to the other kids. "That guy's creeping me out," he said. "There's something weird about him. He doesn't talk. What if he kidnaps us? What if he's really a ghoul and he takes us to his cave and—"

"Ghouls don't live in caves," Ruth Rose said.

"Yeah, they live in graves!" Candy said, raising her voice.

"Hey, Candy, you made a poem!" Adam said.

Dink laughed and lay back in the hay. Suddenly something flew toward the wagon out of the darkness. Dink tried to burrow down into the hay. "Watch out!" he yelled.

"IT'S A WITCH!" Ruth Rose yelled, laughing at the same time. "Watch out, Josh, she's gonna put you in her pot and boil you with a bunch of frogs' eyes!"

"Yummy!" Josh said. "I love frog stew!"

All six kids began laughing and yelling.

The witch flew low over the wagon. She wore a black hat and a flowing cloak. As suddenly as she had appeared, she was gone.

"How did he do that?" Andy asked as they all sat up again.

"Who?" his brother asked.

"The driver," Andy said. "He made those bats attack us, too."

"Maybe he's a magic ghoul!" Josh said.

Everyone laughed.

But they stopped laughing when the wagon pulled up next to a small cemetery. Moonlight and shadows made the place look spooky.

The six kids looked over the side of the wagon. There were only about a dozen tombstones. Most were broken and crumbling on the ground. But there was one new-looking grave marker. The stone stood at the head of an open grave. A pile of dirt was mounded next to the hole.

"This is new," Adam whispered. "There was no grave last year!"

"I don't like this," Candy whispered.

Dink didn't like it, either. He figured

the bats and the witch had been jokes, but this felt different.

Dink started to turn toward the driver, but something caught his eye.

A hand was rising out of the grave! Then came an arm, covered in filthy rags. A second hand and arm appeared, then a face, blotched with dirt. Some of the flesh was peeling off. The hair was ragged, half missing from the awful head.

"I want to go home!" Josh wailed.

The terrible creature crawled from the grave and staggered toward the wagon.

Dink thought he was going to faint. He tried to move, but he had turned to stone.

The man from the grave reached the wagon and jumped onto the ladder.

The kids all screamed as the monster stretched out a hand. He grabbed Dink's ankle and yelled, "FEED ME!"

The driver turned around and bonked the man on the head with a wooden pole. The man fell off the wagon, onto the trail. He sat up, rubbed his head, and called out, "I'm sooooooo huuunnngry!"

The kids watched the man lurch back toward the open grave.

The wagon continued moving.

"Cool!" Andy said. "Did you see that awesome mask?"

"Mask? Was that another trick?" Josh asked.

"Sure," Andy said. "All this stuff is planned, just to scare the heck out of us."

"But he really grabbed me," Dink said. "I could feel his fingers!"

Just then the driver started laughing. He laughed so hard, he had to put down the reins. The horse stopped walking.

The driver rocked in his seat, holding his head and laughing. Suddenly his head flew off his shoulders and landed in the hay between the kids. Red gooey blood oozed from the neck.

The six kids screamed and tried to back away from the head.

"Wait a minute," Adam said. "That's not a real head. It's just a hollow pumpkin!"

"He's right," Josh said. "Look, it's been painted to look like a face!"

"And that's fake blood!" Ruth Rose said.

"That's right," a voice said. The kids looked at the driver. A smiling man was looking back at them. "I'm Officer Klevor. Hope my buddy back there didn't scare you too much."

"That guy from the grave was your friend?" Dink asked.

The driver nodded, grinning. "Yep. That's Officer Reilly. We're both police officers. Ready for the party?"

CHAPTER 4

Officer Klevor flicked the reins, and the horse and wagon began to move again. Minutes later, they came to a wide clearing in the woods. Small lights hung in the trees. Dink could see two other hay wagons parked off to the side. The horses had been unhitched and were grazing. A police cruiser was parked not far from the wagons. The shiny chrome gleamed in the moonlight.

Dink saw a lot of other kids in the clearing. Some wore full costumes, but most just had on masks and were dressed in jeans and sweaters. He

noticed several men and women, all wearing masks or costumes. He saw an Elvis, a clown, and a Humpty Dumpty. He figured they were police officers, too. They were setting up games and placing food on two long tables.

Officer Klevor hopped off the wagon. "Okay, kids, jump down," he said. "We've got games and tons of food, and later there'll be a bonfire." He grinned. "Anyone who doesn't have fun tonight gets arrested!"

The six kids clambered down off the wagon. They wiped hay from their hair and clothing, put on their masks, then ran toward the lights.

"Look," Josh said. He pointed to a group of kids gathered around a boy who had been blindfolded. He was holding a picture of a man's face.

"They're playing pin the head on the headless horseman!" Ruth Rose said. The blindfolded boy staggered forward. Attached to a tree was a picture of a horse with a headless rider.

Everyone in the group laughed when the boy completely missed the tree. One of the police officers whispered something in the boy's ear, then aimed him in the right direction. The police officer was dressed as a spaceman.

Another group of kids were standing

around a barrel of water, dunking for apples.

Other kids were lawn-bowling. Instead of bowling balls, they used small pumpkins.

"Ruth Rose, can I borrow your phone?" Dink asked. "I'd better call my dad."

Ruth Rose dug her cell phone out of her pocket and handed it to Dink. He dialed. "Hi, Dad," he said a few seconds later. "Yeah, we're here, and it's awesome. We got attacked by bats and witches and dead guys crawling out of graves. Oh, and our driver's head fell off! I love this place!"

Dink pushed the button to end the call. He handed the phone back to Ruth Rose. "What do you guys want to do?" he asked.

"Feed me!" Josh said. "I smell hot dogs!"

"I want to dunk for apples," Ruth Rose said. "I'll see you guys in a little while." She headed for the apple dunkers.

"You coming to eat?" Josh asked Dink.

"Not right now," Dink said. "I think I'll try that bowling with pumpkins. It looks like fun."

"Okay, I'll be at the hot dog table," Josh said, grinning. "*That* looks like fun!"

"Don't eat too many," Dink warned.

"How many is too many?" Josh asked.

Dink laughed. "For you, I'd say about twenty!" he said.

Josh made a goofy face at Dink and jogged toward the food. Dink lowered his mask and walked up to a police officer who seemed to be in charge of the pumpkin bowling. The man wore filthy rags and a mask that looked like rotting flesh.

"Hi," Dink said. "Are you the guy from the grave?"

The man lifted his mask away from his face. "I sure am," he said. "But I'm really Officer Reilly. Did I scare you?"

Dink nodded. "Half to death!" he

said. "How'd you get here so fast?"

Officer Reilly pointed to where the cruiser was parked. "As soon as your wagon left, I jumped in and drove here."

"Can I bowl?" Dink asked.

"Sure," Officer Reilly said. "Just grab a pumpkin from that pile over there and get in line."

Dink walked over to the pumpkin pile. He chose a round one, figuring it would roll better.

Holding his pumpkin, Dink stepped in the line of kids waiting to bowl. The kid in front of him was Adam, from the hayride. "Hey," Dink said. "Have you ever done this before?"

Adam turned around and smiled at Dink. "Yeah, my brother and I did it last year. It's crazy! Your pumpkin goes wobbling all over the place. But you only get a prize if you knock over that little ghost statue." Adam pointed.

"There are prizes?" Dink said.

"Yup. Last year I won a little monster that glowed in the dark!" Adam said. "It took me four tries!"

Pretty soon it was Adam's turn to bowl. He stepped up to a rope lying on the grass. With one toe on the rope, Adam tossed his pumpkin using both hands. His pumpkin rolled off into the bushes, missing the ghost statue by five feet!

The other kids in line all laughed. Adam laughed, too, and ran after his pumpkin.

Officer Reilly pointed to Dink. "Your turn," he said. "Good luck!"

Dink decided to try something he'd seen Josh do once when they were in a real bowling alley. He walked up to the rope, but then he turned around so he was facing away from the statue.

"You're bowling backward?" some

other kid asked. "How are you gonna see where your pumpkin is going?"

Holding his pumpkin in both hands, Dink bent over and looked backward through his legs. He could see the statue clearly, but upside down. Then he aimed his pumpkin and hurled it through his legs. It shot straight toward the statue. But at the last second, the pumpkin hit a rock or a bump and flew off in another direction.

"You almost made it, kid!" Officer Reilly said.

Dink lifted his mask and chased after his pumpkin. It had rolled into some bushes growing between a bunch of trees. He finally found the pumpkin in some weeds. As Dink picked it up, he heard a voice somewhere ahead of him. He looked up and saw two dark figures over by the wagons and horses. Even though the moon shone down on them,

Dink couldn't make out the men's faces. *They must be more cops, and they're wearing masks,* Dink thought. The men were patting the horses and talking to them.

Dink noticed something shiny on the ground where the men's feet were. When one of the men moved, the shiny things moved, too. Dink wondered if there were fireflies here at the end of October.

Dink grabbed his pumpkin and trotted back to the clearing. He got in line behind a girl in a Miss Piggy mask. Before it was time for him to bowl again, Josh appeared, chomping on a hot dog.

"Dink, come on, they're starting the bonfire!" Josh said. Dink put his pumpkin back on the pile and followed Josh. The cops had made a circle of tree stumps for the kids to sit on. In the middle, they had piled logs and dry tree branches. An officer lit the pile, and soon it was crackling.

Dink and Josh found Ruth Rose, and the three sat on stumps.

"Did you get an apple?" Dink asked her.

"Yup, and I ate it!" she said. The neck of her sweater and the tips of her hair were wet.

The officer dressed as Elvis passed out marshmallows and pointy sticks. "Wait till the flames die down," he instructed.

It took about five minutes for the dry wood and branches to burn down. Dink, Josh, and Ruth Rose left their masks on the stumps and stepped up to the fire. They reached toward the coals with their marshmallow sticks.

"Guess how many marshmallows I can fit in my mouth at the same time," Josh said.

"A hundred," Dink said. He watched his marshmallow to see that it didn't get too burned.

"Nope. Seventeen," Josh said. "I did it at the twins' birthday party last year. Mom was grossed out. It was so cool!"

"Well, don't do it here," Ruth Rose said. "I don't want to be embarr—"

Just then a girl on the other side of the circle yelled, "Oh my gosh, look!"

Everyone stared at her. No one knew what she was yelling about.

"No, over there!" the girl cried. She pointed into the woods where Dink had chased his pumpkin.

Through the trees, they could all see flames shooting into the sky!

"The hay wagons are burning!" one of the officers yelled.

CHAPTER 5

Everyone started yelling. All the kids jumped off the stumps. Dink saw Officer Klevor yank a cell phone from his pocket. "Fire department, quick!" he yelled into the phone. Then he charged into the woods toward the flames.

The kids all started to follow. Officer Klevor turned around and spread his arms. "No, you kids stay here. We'll take care of this!"

The kids gathered in a group. Dink, Josh, and Ruth Rose found Candy and her two brothers in the crowd. Everyone was talking at once. Josh ate the marsh-mallow off his stick.

"This is amazing!" Andy said. "This never happens in New York City!"

"I wonder if a spark from the bonfire started the hay on fire," Ruth Rose said.

"I bet it was some weirdo who did it just for kicks," Adam said.

Dink suddenly remembered the headless horseman who had ridden past their cabin. He was carrying a jack-o'-lantern. Had it been lit with a candle? Had the horseman come here and burned the wagons?

"What happened to the horses?" Josh asked.

"They must have run away when the fire started," Ruth Rose said.

"How are we supposed to get back to our cabin?" Josh asked.

Even standing where they were, yards from the fire, Dink could feel the heat and smell burning hay and wood. Some of the smoke drifted their way, making his eyes sting.

Then Dink thought about the two men he'd seen near the horses when he'd chased his pumpkin. At the time, he'd thought they were police officers. But were they really cops? Had those men set the fire?

"Somebody will come and get us," Ruth Rose said. "They won't leave a bunch of kids stranded in the woods on Halloween night!"

"It's probably just another trick," Andy said. "The cops faked it to get us real scared. In a minute, they'll probably all bust out laughing."

"You think those burning wagons are fake?" his brother asked. "Get real, Andy!"

Just then they heard a siren in the distance.

"That must be a fire engine!" Josh said.

"They'll never get here in time," Dink said. "Those wagons are burning to the ground."

A few minutes later, two fire engines roared into the clearing. Some of the cops ran to meet them. Dink saw the officer dressed as a spaceman. Every time he took a step, the heels of his sneakers lit up.

Dink's mind flashed again to the two men he'd seen in the woods. One of them had something shiny on his feet. Was this officer dressed as a spaceman one of the two men? Had they burned the wagons? Dink shook the questions away. He must have seen fireflies.

One of the firefighters jumped from his truck to the ground. "What's going on?" he asked the cops.

"Hay wagons on fire," the officer dressed as a space guy answered. "Did you bring water? There are no fire hydrants out here."

"Yeah, we have a full tank," the firefighter said. He climbed back into his truck and drove toward the burning hay wagons.

Officer Klevor came running out of the woods. "That fire is no accident!" he said to the spaceman. "It was deliberately set!"

"How do you know?" his companion asked.

"We found matchbooks on the ground," Officer Klevor said.

Dink and all the other kids watched the firefighters pull hoses and fire extinguishers from the trucks. Minutes later, the flames were gone, replaced by smoke, steam, and a damp smell in the air.

Officer Klevor walked over to the kids. His face was streaked with ashes. "Pretty exciting, eh?" he said. He smiled, but Dink could tell he was upset. His hands shook as he wiped soot from his face. "Let's go back to the circle, kids."

The kids sat on stumps, and Officer Klevor joined them. "The wagons burned up," he said. "But don't worry, we'll get you all home."

"What about the horses?" Josh asked.

"They ran into the woods," Officer

Klevor said. "Officers are out looking for them."

"Who did it?" Adam asked.

Officer Klevor shook his head. "I don't know, but whoever it was is a real jerk," he said.

"Officer Klevor?" Dink said. "I may have seen who set the fires."

Everyone looked at Dink. He felt himself blush.

Officer Klevor asked, "What's your name, son?"

"I'm Dink Duncan," Dink said. "You picked us up at our cabin."

"Oh yeah, you're here with your dad, right?" Officer Klevor asked. "Staying in Haunted House?"

Dink nodded.

"What did you see?" Officer Klevor asked.

"I was bowling, and my pumpkin rolled into the woods," Dink said.

"When I went after it, I saw two men over by the wagons."

"Two men? What did they look like?" Officer Klevor asked.

"I couldn't really see their faces," Dink said. "I think they had Halloween masks on. I thought they were officers, like you."

"What were the men doing?" Officer Klevor asked.

Dink thought back to what he had seen. "They were petting the horses," he said. "At least I think so."

"So you didn't see these men actually set fire to the wagons?"

Dink shook his head. "No. I thought they were just checking on the horses."

Dink decided not to mention that he thought he'd seen something shiny on one of the men's feet. Or that the officer dressed as a spaceman had sneakers that lit up.

Officer Reilly joined them. "We have a problem," he said to Officer Klevor.

"Another one? What is it, Billy?" Officer Klevor asked.

"My cruiser's tires are all flat," he said. "Some crackpot let the air out! So we have no wagons and no car. None of us can leave here."

"You mean we have to stay out in the woods all night?" Josh asked.

CHAPTER 6

Officer Klevor put his hand on Josh's shoulder. "Don't worry, we'll get you back to your cabins," he said. "I called the dispatcher. They promised to get some cars out here as soon as they can."

Officers Klevor and Reilly walked toward the smoldering fire.

Ruth Rose pulled out her cell phone. "You should call your father," she said to Dink.

Dink barely heard her words. He gazed through the trees at what was left of the hay wagons. He saw charred wood on the ground, still smoking. The smell was sharp and putrid, like a dead rabbit he'd once found in the woods in Green Lawn.

Dink was still bothered by the men he'd seen in the woods. Were they police officers? Had they set the wagons on fire? Should he tell Officer Klevor what he suspected about the cop with the sneakers that lit up?

"Dink?" Josh said. "Come back to Earth, dude."

Ruth Rose held her phone out to Dink. "Your dad will be worried when we're late," she said. "You need to call him."

Dink took the phone. He stared at it in his hand. "Sorry, guys, I guess I'm flustered," he said. "I can't even remember his number."

"You don't need the number," Ruth Rose said. She took her phone back and

showed Dink the green *Talk* button.
"Just push this button, and the last
phone number you dialed will ring." She
pushed the button and handed the
phone to Dink.

Dink put the phone to his ear and
heard the ringing. His father answered.

"Dad, hi, it's me," he said. "We're
gonna be a little late getting back."

Josh and Ruth Rose listened as Dink
explained about the fires.

"We're fine, Dad," Dink said into the phone. "They're sending some cars to pick us up. We'll see you later, okay?"

Dink handed the phone back to Ruth Rose.

Josh thumped Dink's shoulder. "Let's go back to the bonfire," he said. "Maybe there are more marshmallows."

Dink, Josh, and Ruth Rose walked back to the circle of stumps. The bonfire was now just hot coals. A few kids were already there, roasting marshmallows. Other kids were sitting on the grass, talking in small groups.

"Who do you suppose set those fires?" Ruth Rose asked.

"Probably those guys Dink saw," Josh said.

"Yeah," Ruth Rose said, "but why would they play such a nasty trick on a bunch of kids they don't even know?"

Dink remembered Officer Reilly

telling Officer Klevor that someone had let the air out of his cruiser tires. That wasn't playing a trick on kids.

Just then four cruisers pulled into the clearing, one behind the other.

The four drivers approached the kids sitting by the bonfire coals.

"Do you kids know where Officer Klevor is?" one of the officers asked.

"He went over there," Dink said, pointing toward the fire engines. He noticed the officer's name tag: OFFICER SNEKE.

"I'm right here, Sam," Officer Klevor said. He had jogged out of the woods.

"What's the deal?" Officer Sneke asked. "We heard there was a fire."

Officer Klevor quickly explained about the burned wagons and the cruiser with flat tires. "Right now, we need to get these kids back to their parents," he said.

"How many kids are there?" Officer Sneke asked.

"About twenty-five, I think," Officer Klevor said. "Can you guys fit them all in?"

"Sure," Officer Sneke said. "If they don't mind being scrunched together."

Officer Klevor smiled. "I think they'd be willing to sit on top of each other if they had to," he said.

"No one's sitting on my lap!" Josh protested.

Everyone laughed.

A few minutes later, all the kids had squeezed into the four cruisers.

Dink, Josh, and Ruth Rose were in the same car with Candy and her two brothers. Officer Sneke was their driver. Candy was sitting on Adam's lap in the back. Andy and Ruth Rose sat next to them. Dink and Josh were in the front with the driver.

Dink watched as the other three cruisers filled with kids pulled away from the bonfire clearing.

Officer Klevor walked up to Officer Sneke's window. "Tell dispatch we need to get an air tank out here," he said. "Billy's tires are all flat."

"Will do," Officer Sneke said. He waved and followed the other cruisers.

Dink glanced at the burned wagons as they passed. He saw an officer walking in the grass near one of the wagons. He seemed to be searching for something. The heels of his sneakers lit up each time he took a step.

Dink recognized the officer who had dressed as a spaceman. What was he looking for?

CHAPTER 7

"What cabins are you kids in?" Officer Sneke asked fifteen minutes later. They were deep in woods that Dink didn't recognize.

"We're in Witch's Hut," Candy said from the backseat. "It's so cool! We found snakes in the bathtub!"

"It's lame," Andy said. "I knew they were rubber."

"Yeah? Then why did you scream?" Adam asked.

"I never screamed," Andy said.

"Did too!" Candy piped up.

"Our cabin is Haunted House," Ruth Rose told Officer Sneke.

"Good, that's just a mile up the road," the officer said. "I'll drop you off first."

A few minutes later, Officer Sneke pulled up to the Haunted House cabin. "Here you go, kids. Have a good sleep," he said.

Dink, Josh, and Ruth Rose hopped out of the cruiser. The front-porch light was on, but the cabin itself was totally dark.

"Good night, you guys," Candy said. "Maybe we'll see you back in town tomorrow."

The kids all said good night, and Officer Sneke pulled away into the black woods.

"Your dad must be asleep," Ruth Rose said quietly. The kids walked up onto the porch. The book that Dink's father had been reading earlier was on the chair, opened. A glass of lemonade stood on the table. It was more than half full. Ice cubes floated in the liquid.

"He told me he'd wait up till we got back," Dink said. He opened the front door. It squeaked, sounding like a scared mouse. "Dad? We're home!"

No one answered. The cabin was dark except for glowing coals in the fireplace. Dink switched on a lamp. The kids blinked when the bright light hit their eyes.

The ticking of the mantel clock was the only sound. It was almost midnight.

"Look," Josh said. He pointed to their sleeping bags. They had been unrolled and lined up near each other on the floor. Three white pillows lay on top of the bags. Chocolate candies shaped like small ghosts had been placed on each pillow.

"Your dad is so cool, Dink!" Ruth Rose said.

"But where is he?" Dink asked. "Dad? Are you here?"

The answer was a slamming door. The kids whipped around to the one they'd just come through.

"Not that door," Ruth Rose whispered. She pointed in front of them, to the closed bedroom door. "The noise came from in there!"

Dink took a deep breath, then slowly opened the bedroom door. "Come on, Dad," he said. "Stop messing around. We know it's Halloween!"

Dink reached into the dark room and flipped the wall switch. The light showed a chair, dresser, and bed. The blankets were in a heap on the floor.

Dink stepped into the room, and the others followed.

"Okay, this is creeping me out," Josh said.

"Listen!" Dink said.

At first they heard nothing but their own breathing, then a low howling filled the room. It got louder, sounding like a hungry wolf. This was followed by scratching fingernails on dry wood.

Ruth Rose giggled. "This is like a scary movie," she whispered to Josh, then raised her voice. "SOMETHING IS BEHIND THAT DOOR!"

Dink gave Josh a little shove. "Open the closet door, Josh," he said. "There might be Halloween candy in there!"

"I wouldn't open that door for all the candy on the planet!" Josh said. "I'm starting to hate Halloween!"

Dink laughed, then walked across the room and yanked open the closet door. A figure draped in a white sheet hopped out.

"BOO!" Dink's father said, pulling the sheet away from his face.

"Hi, Dad," Dink said. "Nice costume."

"It was all I could come up with at the last minute," his father said. He dropped the sheet onto his bed. "Sorry if I scared you."

"We weren't scared!" Josh said.

"Ha!" Ruth Rose said. "Your face was whiter than the sheet!"

"Okay, we all need to get to sleep," Dink's father said. "But first, I want to hear about your night."

Taking turns, the kids told Dink's father what had happened, starting with the bats and witch and ghoul in the woods. Dink's father listened as he made up his bed.

When they got to the part about the burning wagons, he sat on the bed. "That's so strange," he said. "Well, I'm sure the police will figure it out tomorrow. Okay, pajamas and toothbrushing. I'm sure you all ate a lot of candy."

"Josh did," Dink said. "Did you know

he can stuff seventeen marshmallows in his mouth at once?"

"Amazing, Josh!" Mr. Duncan said. "I'd love to see that!"

"Anytime, Mr. Duncan!" Josh said.

Twenty minutes later, the kids were in their sleeping bags. Josh and Ruth Rose were asleep. Dink lay awake, listening to crickets outside the cabin.

Dink rolled over in his sleeping bag and looked out the window. Josh had gobbled up his chocolate ghost, but Dink and Ruth Rose had decided to save theirs. The two miniature ghosts stood on the windowsill. The light from the moon created two ghost shadows on the floor.

Dink wondered—for the hundredth time—who had set the fires. Was it the officer in the spaceman costume? Had those lights come from the heels of his sneakers? There had been two men near the wagons just before they burned: who was the second man?

Maybe I should tell Officer Klevor about the sneaker lights tomorrow, Dink said to himself as he snuggled into the sleeping bag.

Then his eyes popped open. But what if the second man was another cop? What if the other man was Officer Klevor?

CHAPTER 8

The next morning, Dink's dad drove them all to Peach's Pancakes for breakfast. They each ordered a stack of pancakes with sliced fruit on top.

While Dink, Josh, and Ruth Rose cleaned their plates, Dink's father read the local newspaper. "There's nothing in here about the fires last night," he said.

"I guess it happened too late," Dink said. He had decided to find Officer Klevor after breakfast. He'd tell him about the sneakers on one of the men he'd seen near the horses.

A waitress left a check on the table, and Dink's father put some money down. "I was thinking we'd leave for home around noontime," he said. He glanced at his watch. "That gives you a couple of hours to hang around town."

"Thanks, Dad," Dink said. He looked at Josh and Ruth Rose. "Are you guys finished?"

Josh shook his head no and chewed his last bite of pancake.

"I am," Ruth Rose said. She used her napkin. "That was delicious! Thanks a lot, Mr. Duncan."

"You're welcome, Ruth Rose," Dink's dad said.

"Josh, don't lick your plate," Ruth Rose teased. "I'll be embarrassed."

Josh grinned and let out a big sigh. "Thanks, Mr. Duncan," he said. "How many did I eat?"

"Seven," Mr. Duncan said.

"No, it was seventeen," Ruth Rose said.

"Nope, you ate forty-seven," Dink said. "A new world record."

Mr. Duncan stood up. "Okay, I'll see you back at the cabin," he said. "Don't get into any mischief."

Dink's dad headed for the door.

The waitress came to the table and picked up the money. "Will there be anything else?" she asked the three kids.

"What kind of pie do you have?" Josh asked.

Dink and Ruth Rose grabbed Josh and dragged him out of the restaurant.

"But I'm sooo huuunnngry!" Josh said, imitating the grave ghoul they'd met last night.

"Tough," Dink said. "Come on, I want to see if we can find Officer Klevor."

"Why?" Ruth Rose asked.

Dink explained about the strange gleam he'd seen on the feet of one of the men. "It could be an important clue," he added.

"Then why didn't you tell Officer Klevor last night?" Josh asked.

"Because one of the police officers had those sneakers that light up," Dink said. "It might have been him that I saw!"

"So you're thinking maybe one of the officers set fire to the wagons?" Josh asked.

"Yeah," Dink answered glumly.

"But why would a police officer want to burn the wagons?" Ruth Rose asked.

"That's what I want to know," Dink said.

The kids headed up Main Street. They asked a woman walking her dog

where the police station was.

"It's near the library," the woman said. "Just keep going straight on Main Street."

But they never made it to the police

station. Two police cruisers raced past them with their lights flashing.

"Where the heck are they going?" Josh asked.

"Let's find out!" Ruth Rose said. She began sprinting up Main Street. Dink and Josh ran after her.

They didn't have to go far. In front of the bank, the cruisers were blocking the street. Two police officers were guarding the door. Two other officers came out of the bank. One of the officers was Officer Klevor. He was carrying a length of yellow rope. Between the two cops was the woman who had started the mechanical horse in the bank window yesterday.

The woman was crying.

"Tell us what happened, Bonnie," Officer Klevor said gently.

"They came to my home last night," she said between sobs. "It was nearly midnight. They made me put on my coat and shoes, then brought me here to the bank. They said they wanted the money from the vault. They knew a lot of money came in yesterday. But I told them I couldn't open the vault. It opens automatically at eight every morning."

"Did they believe you about the vault?" Officer Klevor asked.

The woman nodded. "I tried to get them to just leave, but they tied me up. They used that rope. Then they took money from the tellers' drawers and left."

"How much money was in the drawers?" asked Officer Klevor.

"Not much, two hundred dollars maybe," the woman said.

"Did you recognize the men?" Officer Klevor asked.

Bonnie shook her head. "They wore masks, like for Halloween," she said. Then she burst into tears again.

A man in a business suit came out of the bank. He walked over to the officers and Bonnie. "Please go home until you feel better," he told the woman. "I'll take care of things here."

"Thank you, Mr. Garth," Bonnie said. "Oh, and I called the party company to come and get the mechanical horse. They should be here soon."

"Thank you, Bonnie," Mr. Garth said. "Don't worry about that. Just get some rest."

Officer Klevor noticed Dink, Josh, and Ruth Rose. He nodded as he helped Bonnie into his cruiser. They sped away, followed by the other car.

"Wow," Josh said. "The bank got robbed while we were at the bonfire party!"

"I'll bet that's why those two guys set the fire last night," Dink said. "They wanted the cops stuck in the woods while they made Bonnie open the bank for them. The guys who robbed the bank must be the same guys who burned the wagons!"

Just then an orange pickup truck pulled up. A sign on its side said RIDE 'EM, COWBOY—RIDE US AT YOUR NEXT PARTY. There was a picture of a cowboy riding a bucking horse.

Two men got out of the truck and walked up to the bank. One was tall with broad shoulders. The other was short and chubby. They wore gray work shirts with RIDE 'EM, COWBOY patches sewn onto the sleeves. They disappeared inside the bank.

"Look," Josh said. He pointed at the bank window.

The men appeared in front of the curtain. One of them unplugged an electric cord that ran from the horse's belly to an outlet in the wall. Then both men picked up the horse and moved it through the curtain. A minute later, they were on the sidewalk, carrying the horse and its headless rider between them.

"Careful with this baby," the taller man said. "It's worth a lot of money."

"Got it," the other man said.

The men loaded the horse into the back of the truck.

"Lay it on its side," the tall man said.

When the horse and rider were flat on the truck bed, one of the men pulled a blue tarp from the passenger seat. The men unfolded the tarp and threw it over the horse and rider, hiding them from view. They used yellow rope to tie the tarp to the sides of the truck.

"I need a coffee to go," the chubby man said.

"Okay, but make it snappy," his buddy said.

They walked into the ice cream shop.

Dink thought he'd heard those

voices before. And he was positive he'd
seen the tall man's cowboy boots yesterday afternoon. He'd stepped on one of
them. The boots had silver toes. Shiny
silver toes.

Suddenly Dink raced over to the
truck. He lifted a corner of the tarp and
climbed up onto the truck bed.

"Dink, what're you doing?" Josh
asked. He and Ruth Rose ran over to the
truck.

"Tell me if they come out!" Dink
said. Hidden by the tarp, he opened the
little door on the horse's side. He
reached his arm inside. His fingers
touched cloth bags, and he knew what
was inside the bags.

"Dink, what's going on?" Ruth Rose
asked.

"I found the money!" Dink whispered back.

CHAPTER 9

Twenty seconds later, Josh and Ruth Rose were climbing under the tarp with Dink.

"Look," Dink said. He reached inside the horse's stomach and pulled out one of the bags.

"Is that what I think it is?" Ruth Rose asked.

Dink nodded. "Remember, we saw those guys bringing it into the bank yesterday?" he asked.

"You mean, that's all money?" Josh gulped.

"Yeah, and there are about ten more

bags inside the horse," Dink said.

"Holy moly!" Josh gasped. "How'd it get there?"

"I'm not sure," Dink replied. He thought for a minute. "Maybe the robbers put it there," he said.

"But that woman—Bonnie—told the police that they only took two hundred dollars," Ruth Rose said. "There must be a lot more than that in only one of these bags!"

"Then she wasn't telling the truth," Dink said. "But why?"

"Wait a minute!" Josh said. "Maybe Bonnie is one of the crooks. She could've hid the money in the horse. And—"

"You're right!" Dink said. "She must have taken the money out of the vault this morning, after it opened automatically!"

Just then they heard the truck's

doors open. The truck rocked as someone climbed into the cab, and the doors slammed, one after the other. Then the engine roared.

When the truck started moving, Dink thought he was going to be sick. The three of them were trapped in the truck!

The ride was noisy and bumpy.

"What are we gonna do?" Josh asked. His head was scrunched up next to Dink's elbow.

"I don't know," Dink said. It was hot under the tarp. Sweat ran into his eyes, making them sting.

"Well, I do!" Ruth Rose said. She was curled up like a pretzel near Josh's knees. She pulled out her cell phone. "I'm calling Officer Klevor!"

"Call nine-one-one," Dink said. "It'll be faster!"

Ruth Rose tapped in the three digits.

She shook her head at the boys. Then she tried it again. "Nothing," she whispered. "I can't get any signal."

"Maybe we can jump out," Josh said.

"No, we're going too fast," Dink said. "But I have an idea!"

He grabbed a bag of money and untied the twine that kept it closed. Then he yanked out a fistful of money and handed it to Josh. "Throw this out the back of the truck," he said.

"What? Are you crazy?" Josh cried.

"We'll leave a money trail," Dink explained. "People will see it, and maybe

they'll call the cops. The money could lead them to this truck!"

"That's a great idea!" Ruth Rose said. She pulled a handful of bills from the bag and slipped her hand under the edge of the tarp. "I did it!" she said. "I threw money away!"

The kids pulled all the money out of the bag and dropped it under the tarp, out of the truck.

"What if those guys up front see the money flying around?" Josh said.

"If they do, they'll stop," Dink said. "Then maybe we can get away."

RIDE 'EM, COWBOY

RIDE US AT
YOUR NEXT PARTY

Then he had another idea. "Ruth Rose, do you have a marker in your book bag?" he asked.

"Of course," she said. She opened a small zippered pocket. "What color?"

"Any color, but quick!" Dink said.

Ruth Rose handed Dink a blue marker.

Dink grabbed it and scrawled CALL THE POLICE on the empty money bag. He tossed the bag out of the truck.

A minute later, the truck swerved, then slowed. It stopped. Dink put his fingers to his lips. *Maybe,* he thought, *they'll leave the truck, and we can hop out and run away.*

Dink heard the men walking near the side of the truck.

"Let's get this baby inside," a voice said. The voice was only ten inches from Dink's ear.

Suddenly the tarp was yanked away.

Bright sunlight made the kids squint. The truck was parked in front of a barn behind an old house. The yard was full of weeds. An old car sat on cinder blocks because it had no tires.

Two men stared down at the kids.

"What're you little rats doing?" one of them asked. It was the tall man.

Dink couldn't say a word. He thought he'd swallowed his tongue.

"Ace, look," the chubby man said. He pointed to the opened door in the horse's side. "They know about the money!"

"I can see that for myself, Goose," Ace said. He stared at the kids. "All right, who are you? How'd you get in this truck?"

"Never mind who we are!" Ruth Rose shouted. "Let us go, or I'm calling the cops!" She showed the men her cell phone.

Ace reached for the phone, but Ruth Rose dropped it on the truck bed. Dink grabbed the phone and started to punch in a number.

Ace snatched the phone out of Dink's hands. "Now what, little boy?" he asked as he slipped the phone into his shirt pocket.

Dink recognized the man's voice. He looked down and saw silver toes on cowboy boots. "You set the wagons on fire last night!" Dink said.

Ace smirked. "Yep, and my buddy Goose let the air out of that cop's tires," he said.

"Kept those guys busy, didn't it?" said Goose. "Now we got a surprise for you kids. Right, Ace?"

"Right. Let's stash 'em in the barn," Ace said. "Then we'll paint the truck and get out of here."

The chubby man reached for Josh.

"Watch it, buddy," Josh said. He held up his hands. "I know karate!"

"Me too," Goose said. "And I'm bigger than you."

The men yanked the kids out of the truck. They marched them into the barn.

"Put 'em down there," Ace said. He pointed to a hole in the barn floor.

"I'm afraid of dark places," Josh said. "I'll throw up."

"Sorry about that," Ace said. One by one, he and Goose lowered the three kids by their arms into the deep hole.

Dink, Josh, and Ruth Rose crouched in the dark space. It was an underground room with a dirt floor and walls. Old tin cans and bottles lay everywhere. Some still had stuff in them. The smell of rotting food and damp dirt nearly made Dink gag.

"Enjoy your stay in Barn Hole

Hotel!" Goose yelled down at them.

"You'll never get away!" Ruth Rose yelled up at the men. "People know we're here! They'll come and find us!"

"In your dreams, little girl," Goose said. "But don't worry, when we're a hundred miles away, we'll use your cute little cell phone to let the cops know where we stashed you."

Then the kids watched in horror as he slid something solid over the hole. Now they were in pitch-darkness.

They heard the men's footsteps as they crossed the barn floor above. Then there was just black silence.

A few seconds later, they heard a motor, and something heavy shook the floor above their heads.

"It's the truck," Dink said. "They must have brought it into the barn to paint it."

"I feel so stupid for letting that guy

get my cell phone," Ruth Rose said. "Now what're we going to do?"

"Guys, I have something to tell you," Dink said. "Let's sit down."

"Where?" Josh asked. "This floor is nasty!"

"Move some of this junk out of the way," Dink said. "Toss it in a corner."

Dink could hear Josh fumbling and muttering in the dark a few feet away.

Suddenly Ruth Rose gasped.

"What's wrong?" Dink asked.

"I touched someone," Ruth Rose said. Her voice was trembling. "I think it was a . . . body!"

CHAPTER 10

"I hope you're kidding," Josh said. "It's a Halloween joke, right?"

"I'm not kidding," Ruth Rose said. "I felt skin!"

Dink followed Ruth Rose's voice. He put his hand on her shoulder. "Where?" he asked.

Ruth Rose took Dink's hand and stretched out his arm. Dink's fingers felt clothing, like a shirt. Moving his hands, he felt another pair of hands and rope wound around them. He moved his hand up and felt a face. Then his fingers touched something smooth, not skin. It was tape.

The mouth behind the tape made a choking sound.

"Guys, there's someone tied up and gagged down here," Dink said. "Help me get him loose!"

Dink worked on the tape. He found a corner and carefully pulled it away.

"Thanks, man!" a hoarse voice said. "I could hardly breathe!"

"Who are you?" Dink asked.

"I'm Hank. Those two guys who tossed you in here stole my truck," the man said.

"The Ride 'Em, Cowboy truck?" Ruth Rose asked.

"Yes. I was supposed to go to the bank and pick up one of my mechanical horses," Hank said. "They jumped me and drove me here. I've been in this stinking hole for hours! Can you get these ropes off?"

Dink tried loosening the knots at the man's wrists, but couldn't. "These knots are too tight!" he said.

Ruth Rose got her knife out of her book bag. "Here, try this," she said, handing the knife to Dink.

Just then they heard a loud motor over their heads.

"Are they leaving?" Josh asked.

"No, they're using a paint sprayer on the truck," Hank said. "I hope they chose a good color."

Dink opened a blade in Ruth Rose's knife. Soon the ropes were off, and Hank sat up in the dark. "Thanks, kid," he said. "Who are you, anyway?"

Dink explained who they were and why they'd hidden in the truck.

"So they robbed the bank and hid the money inside my horse?" Hank asked the kids.

"Yeah, and they're gonna get away with it!" Josh said.

"Maybe not," Dink said. "The cops might be here by then."

"What cops?" Josh asked. "The police think the robbers took off last night!"

"And how would the cops find us, anyway?" Hank asked.

Dink grinned in the dark. "My dad will tell them," he said.

"Your dad?" Josh asked. "He doesn't even know where we are!"

"That's what I started to tell you when Ruth Rose found Hank," Dink said. "Before that jerk grabbed Ruth Rose's phone, I hit the green *Talk* button. That would have dialed my dad's number, right, Ruth Rose? And Dad would have heard what those guys said to us, so he'd know we've been kidnapped. He'd call the cops."

"And maybe they'll see the money we threw out of the truck," Ruth Rose said. She explained to Hank how they'd emptied one of the stolen bags.

"Cool idea," Hank said.

"What if your dad didn't answer his phone?" Josh asked Dink. "What if he left it somewhere or went out for a walk without it?"

Dink felt his stomach clench like a fist. He hadn't thought of that. Of course, if his dad didn't hear the phone ring, he wouldn't answer it. And he wouldn't hear what any of them said

before they were lowered into the hole.

"He usually keeps it with him," Dink said. But he was worried.

"Let's just cool it," Hank said. "My partner must be wondering where I am right about now. When I don't get back, he'll call the cops."

Hank and the kids sat against one of the dirt walls.

"I wonder if this place has room service," Josh said. "I need cookies and milk."

Ruth Rose giggled in the dark. "Dink, how did you figure it out?" she asked. "How did you know the money was inside the horse?"

"The guy they call Ace is wearing cowboy boots with silver toes," Dink answered. "I saw him yesterday in front of the bank. And the rope he used to tie the tarp over the horse was the same rope that woman Bonnie was tied up with. And yesterday, when we were watching the mechanical horse, he said

something about Bonnie filling it with
green candy."

"Green candy is money," Josh said.

Dink thought for a minute. "Last
night before the fire, I saw two guys
near the horses," he said. "One of them
had something shiny on his feet. At first
I thought it was that cop who was
dressed as a spaceman. He was wearing
sneakers with heels that lit up. But now
I realize what I saw was the silver tips
on Ace's cowboy boots."

"So you figured out it was an inside
job?" Hank said.

"Right," Dink said. "I think Bonnie
was lying when she told the police that
the men kidnapped her late last night.
I'll bet she let them inside early this
morning. When the vault opened at
eight o'clock, they hid the money inside
the horse. Then they tied Bonnie up to
make it look like she was innocent."

"She knew her boss would come

pretty soon and find her, right?" Josh asked.

"Yeah, but by the time they figured everything out, Ace and Goose would be far away with the money," Dink said. "She's probably going to meet them somewhere."

"But I still don't understand why they burned the hay wagons last night," Josh said.

"The way I figure, they wanted the cops to think the bank was robbed late at night, while we were all stuck in the woods," Dink said. "Bonnie told Officer Klevor that the crooks came at midnight and took only a small amount of money, then left. The police would figure the crooks had over eight hours to get away and wouldn't bother going after them."

"Wow, that was some plan," Hank said. "When the real plan was to hide the bags of money in the horse after the vault opened this morning."

"Right," Dink said. "Bonnie must have told Ace and Goose that you were coming to pick up your horse. So they decided to take your truck so *they* could get the horse."

"You got that right," Hank said. "They jumped me outside my house. Made me spill my coffee! Next thing I knew, I was in this hole."

Suddenly the paint sprayer motor stopped.

"What's going on?" Josh whispered.

"Either they finished the paint job or they ran out of paint," Hank said.

The four prisoners sat in the dark, listening. They heard nothing.

Dink had an idea. "Hank, can I stand on your shoulders?" he asked.

CHAPTER 11

"Sure, kid," Hank said. "You got a plan?"

"Yes," Dink said. "If I can move whatever they used to cover the hole, maybe I can run to town and get the police."

"And leave us here?" Josh said.

"I don't know what else we can do," Dink said. "If we just stay here, they'll get away with the money. We don't know how long it will take the police to find us."

"Yeah, maybe they were lying about letting the police know where we are,"

Ruth Rose said. "They lied about everything else!"

"Okay, kid," Hank said. "It's worth a try."

Dink heard Hank position himself. "Okay, step on my knee, then I'll hoist you up," Hank said.

A minute later, Dink was standing on Hank's shoulders. Hank held Dink's hands so he wouldn't topple off. Dink felt like an acrobat in a circus.

"You okay?" Hank asked.

Dink licked his lips. "Yeah, only I feel like I'm gonna fall."

"You're fine. I won't let you fall. Can you reach the top?" Hank asked. "I'll let go of one of your hands, all right?"

"Okay," Dink said. He felt Hank release his right hand. Suddenly he lost his balance. "Hank, I'm falling!"

"Grab my head!" Hank said.

Dink's free hand found the top of

Hank's head, and he held on.

"Okay, you want to try again?" Hank asked.

"I'm ready," Dink said. With his left hand still clutching Hank's left hand, he reached his right hand straight up. His fingers swept the air blindly, feeling nothing.

Then they made contact.

"I think I'm touching the top!" Dink whispered.

"What is it?" Hank asked. "Can you lift it up?"

Dink dragged his fingertips along something rough and solid. He pushed, and the flat object lifted, but only slightly.

"I think it's wood. Hank, I need both hands," Dink said.

He felt Hank release his other hand. Then Dink felt Hank's strong hands clamp on to his knees.

"Go for it, kid," Hank said. "I've got you."

Slowly, Dink reached both hands over his head. He felt himself swaying in the dark, but when he had two hands pressing against the wood, he regained his balance.

Dink steadied his feet on Hank's shoulders. He took a breath and slowly pushed upward with his hands. It felt like the thin plywood he, Josh, and Ruth

Rose used to build a tree house in Josh's backyard.

The flat wood lifted a few inches. For a moment, Dink was blinded by sunlight. The stink of fresh paint stung his nostrils.

He squinted and looked across the barn floor. He saw old farm tools and clumps of hay. He saw the rear of the truck, not far from the edge of the hole. Turning his head, Dink saw the mechanical horse on its side. He wondered if the money was still inside. The blue tarp was in a heap near the horse.

Dink peered under the truck, between the tires. He had a clear view of the old house. On its steps sat Ace and Goose. Several bank bags were on the ground. They were counting the money!

No way am I going to be able to run for help, Dink said to himself. He knew they'd grab him before he took two steps.

Then Dink made another discovery. One of the truck tires was only inches from his fingers. He smiled at his new idea, glad he'd hung on to Ruth Rose's knife.

He gently let the wood down and rested his arms against its bottom surface. "Hank," he whispered.

"Yeah, kid?"

"Does your truck have a spare tire?" Dink asked.

Hank chuckled. "Nope. Been meaning to get one. . . ."

"I need one of those tin cans on the floor," Dink said.

Hank relayed the message to Josh and Ruth Rose.

Dink heard his friends scurrying in the dark to find a can.

"Coming up," Hank said a minute later.

Dink slowly reached one hand down and took a tin can from Hank.

He lifted the wood again and used the can to prop it open. Then he eased the knife from his pocket.

Dink slid his arm out past the can. He pushed the tip of the knife blade against the truck's rubber tire.

CHAPTER 12

But he couldn't do it. His plan had been to slash a tire so Ace and Goose couldn't drive away with the money. But this was Hank's truck and Hank's tires. *Why should I ruin a perfectly good tire?* Dink asked himself.

Dink had another idea. He folded away the knife blade and flipped out a tiny screwdriver. He held the knife in his right hand. With his left, he reached out and unscrewed the little cap over the tire's air valve. Then he inserted the tip of the screwdriver into the valve and pushed.

He heard air escaping from the tire. He hoped that the two crooks didn't hear the hissing noise.

When the tire was flat, Dink shoved the knife into his pocket. He removed the tin can and began to lower the plywood. Then, from the corner of his eye, he saw something interesting: the yellow rope Ace and Goose had used to secure the tarp over the mechanical horse. It was in a loose pile near the truck's rear tire.

Dink reached an arm out of the hole and grabbed the rope. He tied one end of the rope to the truck's bumper. He yanked on it to tighten the knot. Then he dropped the rest of the rope down into the hole.

He lowered the plywood. "Hank, I'm coming down," he whispered.

Dink felt Hank's hands leave his knees. "I've got you."

A few seconds later, Dink was kneeling on the damp floor of the hole. Once again, he felt blind.

"What did you see up there?" Ruth Rose asked.

"They're counting the money," Dink said. "There's an old house and a yard. Hank, your truck is red now."

"What's with the rope?" Hank asked.

"I tied it to the truck," Dink said. "I thought maybe you could climb up the rope, Hank. Then you could pull us out."

"Awesome!" Josh said. "This is better than TV!"

"It might work," Hank said. "Where are those guys? Will they see me?"

"I don't think they will," Dink said. "They're over by the house. Your truck is between this hole and them."

"Okay, I'm tying a loop in the end of this rope," Hank said. "After I'm up, you kids can put your feet into the loop, and

I'll pull you up, one at a time."

Hank tugged the rope tight, then began climbing, hand over hand, with his legs and feet helping him.

Dink heard him grunting. He remembered trying to climb a thick rope in gym class. It wasn't easy!

A moment later, Dink, Josh, and Ruth Rose saw daylight as Hank moved the plywood. They saw him scramble up and out onto the barn floor.

Dink found the end of the rope and held out the loop. "Who's going first?" he asked.

"You go," Ruth Rose said. "You did all the work."

"No, let Josh go," Dink said. "He's the strongest, so he can help Hank pull us up."

"I think Ruth Rose should go first," Josh said. "She's afraid of the dark."

"I am not afraid of the dark, Joshua

Pinto!" Ruth Rose said. She thrust the loop at him. "Go on up."

Dink figured Josh was just being nice. Everyone knew Josh hated dark places. "Go, Josh!" he said.

Josh stuck a foot into the loop. The rope became taut as Hank hauled up the extra length. Josh held on to the rope with both hands. Dink and Ruth Rose watched as he rose toward Hank.

"Your turn," Dink said after they saw Hank lift Josh out of the hole.

"Are you sure?" Ruth Rose asked.

Dink grinned. "I love dark, smelly places," he said.

Then Ruth Rose followed Josh up. Dink could hear Hank's deep breaths as he hauled on the rope, now carrying Ruth Rose's weight.

For the last time, the looped end of the rope fell at Dink's feet.

But before Dink could put a foot into

the loop, the yellow rope came slicing through the air, landing on Dink's head and shoulders. It was no longer tied to the truck's bumper!

Dink stared straight up. Who had untied the rope—or cut it—and dropped it down into the hole? Where were Josh and Ruth Rose and Hank?

Suddenly Dink heard a man's voice shout. Then he heard more yells. Surely that was Ruth Rose's loud scream!

Dink thought he heard cars arriving.

There were thudding footsteps on the barn floor. And more yelling—this time Dink was sure it was Josh.

Then came silence.

Dink stared at the escape hole above his head. He saw dust floating in the sunlight. He heard only a lonely bird-call, then nothing.

Dink sat on the damp floor. He held the rope in his hands. He closed his eyes, hoping that when he opened them he would see Hank's face looking back at him.

He heard footsteps and looked up. Part of the light was blocked by a man's head and shoulders.

"Dink?" a familiar voice said. "Your friend Josh tells me maple walnut is your favorite ice cream. Why don't I send a ladder down for you, then we'll go get some?"

Dink grinned. "Thanks, Officer Klevor," he said.

A few hours later, Dink, Josh, and Ruth Rose were on their way back to Connecticut. Dink's father drove slowly through town, heading for the highway.

"Look, the bank is closed," Josh said, pointing out the window.

"Yes, they need to hire a new teller," Dink's father said. "Miss Bonnie is behind bars with her brother, Ace, and Goose."

"I'm glad you had your cell phone with you, Mr. Duncan," Ruth Rose said.

"Me too," he said. "I knew the call was coming from your cell phone. So when I heard a man's voice, I was shocked. I was able to hear everything Ace and Goose said, even after they put you in the hole. I drove to the police station with my phone to my ear!"

"How much money did they hide inside the horse?" Josh asked.

"Officer Klevor told me it was about a half-million dollars," Mr. Duncan said.

The three kids gasped.

"Did they find the money we threw away?" Josh asked.

"Some of it," Dink's father said. He smiled. "I'll bet a lot of people will be finding money for quite a while."

Just then Dink saw three familiar

kids on the sidewalk. "Dad, can you stop for a minute?" he asked.

Dink's father pulled over.

"It's those kids we met last night," Dink said. Dink, Josh, and Ruth Rose climbed out of the car.

Candy and her two brothers ran up to them. "Hi, you guys!" she said. "Guess what I just found?" She held up a fifty-dollar bill. "It was just lying by the side of the road!"

"Boy, are you lucky!" Ruth Rose said.

"We're gonna make her split it with us," Adam said. "Right, Andy?"

The other boy nodded. "It's the only interesting thing that happened in this boring town. I can't wait to get back home."

"We're leaving, too," Josh said, poking Dink. "Nothing ever happens around here."

The six kids slapped high fives and

said good-bye to each other. Dink, Josh, and Ruth Rose got back in the car, and Dink's father pulled away from the curb.

"Will they have to return the money?" Dink asked his dad.

"Probably, if the bank decides to let the public know how the money got thrown out of the truck," he said. "Speaking of which, there may be a reward for you three."

"Really?" Josh said. "Awesome!"

"Dad, did the police say if they found the wagon horses?" Dink asked. "They ran away last night during the fire."

Dink's father nodded. "Yep, all three horses are back with their owners," he said. "And the farmers all had insurance, so they'll get money to buy new wagons."

"This is the best Halloween I have

ever had!" Dink said, smiling.

"It was the scariest, that's for sure," Ruth Rose said.

"There's one thing I don't understand," Josh said.

Dink's father looked at Josh in the rearview mirror. "What's that, Josh?" he asked.

"Who was riding the horse we saw out our window last night, before the hay wagon came?" Josh asked. "You know, the headless dude."

"Gee, Josh, I have no idea," Mr. Duncan said.

"Maybe it was one of the town cops," Ruth Rose said. "Officer Klevor pretended to lose his head on the wagon, remember?"

"I asked Officer Klevor when we were at the police station," Dink said. "He told me the headless horseman wasn't one of his officers."

"Then who was it?" Josh asked. "A ghost?"

No one in the car said anything. Mr. Duncan pulled onto the highway and headed for home.

A to Z Mysteries

Dear Readers,

When I was about ten years old, I had a friend who lived on a farm. I spent a lot of time there after school and on weekends. His family grew corn, strawberries, and pumpkins. They also had a barn filled with farm animals. We used to play with the baby goats, feed the chickens, and try to milk Carol, the brown cow.

But our favorite animal on the farm was Doc, a huge workhorse. Doc lived in the barn with Carol and the chickens and goats. There were cats in the barn, too. Some of them slept in the hay next to Doc and Carol and the goats.

On weekends, my friend's father would hitch Doc up to a wagon and give all us kids rides. On really hot days, we'd ride to the river and take a swim. Doc would stand on the riverbank and drink what seemed like gallons of water!

One October my friend told me that his dad was going to have a hayride. He filled the wagon behind Doc with soft hay. When it grew dark, he hitched Doc up, and off we went. What I didn't know was that my friend and his dad planned to scare us! They had hung ghosts and witches and other scary stuff from the trees. I'll never forget seeing those creepy things as Doc pulled the wagon beneath the branches. Of course, I didn't know then that someday I would put that experience into this book. I hope you enjoyed the scary ride!

Happy reading!

Sincerely,

Ron Roy

P.S. Be sure to look for the answer to the hidden message on the bottom of the next page. And please keep visiting my Web site at www.ronroy.com!

Did you find the secret message hidden in this book?

If you *don't* want to know the answer, *don't* look at the bottom of this page!

Answer: THE HEADLESS HORSEMAN RIDES ON

The alphabet may be over, but the A to Z Mysteries fun just keeps on coming!

How many of KC and Marshall's adventures have you read?

Capital Mysteries

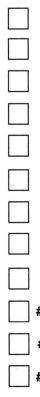

☐ #1 Who Cloned the President?

☐ #2 Kidnapped at the Capital

☐ #3 The Skeleton in the Smithsonian

☐ #4 A Spy in the White House

☐ #5 Who Broke Lincoln's Thumb?

☐ #6 Fireworks at the FBI

☐ #7 Trouble at the Treasury

☐ #8 Mystery at the Washington Monument

☐ #9 A Thief at the National Zoo

☐ #10 The Election-Day Disaster

☐ #11 The Secret at Jefferson's Mansion

☐ #12 The Ghost at Camp David

Track down all these books or a little mystery in your life!

A to Z Mysteries®
by Ron Roy

Capital Mysteries
by Ron Roy
Who Cloned the President?
Kidnapped at the Capital
The Skeleton in the Smithsonian
A Spy in the White House
Who Broke Lincoln's Thumb?
Fireworks at the FBI
Trouble at the Treasury
Mystery at the Washington Monument
A Thief at the National Zoo
The Election-Day Disaster
The Secret at Jefferson's Mansion
The Ghost at Camp David

The Case of the Elevator Duck
by Polly Berrien Berends

Ghost Horse
by George Edward Stanley

**If you like the A to Z Mysteries,
you might want to read**

GHOST HORSE
by George Edward Stanley

Emily got out of bed. She ran to the window and pulled back the curtains. In the moonlight, she could see the beautiful white horse!

Emily pinched herself. "Ouch!" Now she knew she wasn't dreaming. The beautiful white horse was really there!

He started walking toward her window. But the closer he got, the paler he got.

Emily gasped. She could see through the horse!

"You're . . . you're a ghost!" she whispered.